MW00915344

Peanut and Pearl's Picnic Adventure

story by Rebecca Kai Dotlich
pictures by R. W. Alley

HarperCollins*Publishers*

 Printed in the United States of America. For information address HarperCollins Children's Books, a division of HarperCollins Publishers, 1350 Avenue of the Americas, New York, NY 10019. www.harpercollinschildrens.com

Library of Congress Cataloging-in-Publication Data is available.
ISBN-10: 0-06-054920-3 — ISBN-13: 978-0-06-054920-6
ISBN-10: 0-06-054921-1 (lib. bdg.) — ISBN-13: 978-0-06-054921-3 (lib. bdg.)

1 2 3 4 5 6 7 8 9 10 ❖ First Edition

For two double-fine characters:
Anne Hoppe and Simone Kaplan,
with gratitude and affection
—R.K.D.

For Anne Hoppe,
friend and editor
—R.W.A.

Meet Peanut.

He likes cowboy hats.

Hello, Peanut!

Meet Pearl.

She likes party hats.

Hello, Pearl!

"Let's go on a picnic,"
says Pearl.

“Yes!” says Peanut.

Peanut packs a lunch.
He packs corn cakes.

Pearl packs a lunch.
She packs plum pie.

Peanut leads the way.

Pearl leads the way.

Peanut looks around.

No Pearl.

"Pearl is lost," says Peanut.

Pearl looks around.

No Peanut.

"Peanut is lost," says Pearl.

Peanut eats corn cakes.
Peanut takes a nap.

Pearl eats plum pie.
Pearl does not take a nap.
Pearl looks for Peanut.

Pearl looks behind
the smallest tree.
No Peanut.

Pearl looks behind
the biggest tree.
No Peanut.

Pearl looks by the lake.
"There you are, Peanut!"
says Pearl.

“Pearl!” says Peanut.

“You were lost.”

“YOU were lost,”

says Pearl.

Peanut shakes his head.
“I was right where I was,”
says Peanut.

Pearl shakes her head.
"I was right where *I* was,"
says Pearl.

"We were both lost,"
says Peanut.
Peanut and Pearl laugh.

"I love picnics,"
says Peanut.

"Me too!"
says Pearl.

"Next time, I will pack cupcakes," says Peanut.

“Next time, I will pack a map,” says Pearl.

“You better pack two maps,”
says Peanut.

Pearl

"Good idea," says Pearl.
"Picnics are more fun
with two!"